A Tale of Two Kitties

by Liz Pichon

SCHOLASTIC
PRESS

This is the tale of two very different kitties.

Fluffy and Scruffy were neighbours, but they were certainly NOT friends.

Fluffy thought that Scruffy was revolting and lazy.

Scruffy thought that Fluffy was far too tidy and no fun at all.

Fluffy lived in a house that was spotlessly clean.

Scruffy's house was messy and disgusting.

Fluffy's fur was always sleek and lovely.

She kept her claws beautifully trimmed and neat.

Scruffy loved to roll around in MUCK.

His fur was smelly and grimy and his claws were FILTHY.

Fluffy ate delicious food from a delicate china bowl.

Scruffy ate absolutely EVERYTHING he could, wherever he found it.

Fluffy liked to keep busy (mostly grooming and tidying).

Scruffy was extremely lazy and would sleep as much as possible.

You couldn't have found two more different kitties if you'd tried.

One day, a small family of mice was

looking for a new place to live.

They saw Scruffy's house and thought,

"Nice place, let's move in."

So they did.

The mice quickly made themselves at home.

They ate leftovers and rolled around in muck.

They messed the house up even more.

"This place is FUN!" the mice laughed.

And it was . . . until Scruffy woke up.

It's true, Scruffy was LAZY and DISGUSTING.

But he was also the fastest mouse chaser EVER!

He chased the mice around the house, out to the garden,

over the wall and right into Fluffy's house.

"Ha ha," smiled Scruffy. "Let's see how Miss Fluffy Paws

deals with all those messy mice!"

puff
puff

Run for it!

Fluffy was HORRIFIED.

At first she tried to chase the mice, but with her neat and tidy claws she was too slow.

"This is too much," sighed Fluffy.

"I am far too clean and gorgeous to chase those horrid little mice any more!"

So Fluffy decided the only thing to do was to . . .

. . . **COMPLETELY** ignore them!

The mice were delighted. They were having the time of their lives.

They raided the fridge. They danced until dawn.

More and more and more mice came to join in the fun.

After the mice had scoffed all of Fluffy's delicious food,

they sang rude songs (really loudly). It kept Fluffy awake ALL night long.

So she moved out of her noisy house and into the garden.

"Mice are not nice," Fluffy said sadly.

The mice were SO loud, even Scruffy couldn't sleep.

When he saw Fluffy in the garden, he actually felt sorry for her.

"Those mice are getting on my nerves," said Scruffy.

"There are too many mice for me to chase on my own," said Fluffy.

So Fluffy and Scruffy agreed that together they would get rid

of those mice once and for all. . .

First, Fluffy rolled in muck to disguise herself as Scruffy.

Next, Scruffy cleaned himself up to look more like Fluffy.

Now both cats were ready to trick those messy mice.

They crept back into the house to put their clever plan into action.

Fluffy hid under the stairs while Scruffy went to find the mice.

The mice didn't recognise Scruffy at all.

"We're too fast for you!" they said cheekily.

They ran downstairs and into what they
thought was a safe, dark corner.

"BIG MISTAKE!" shouted Fluffy
as she slammed shut the lid of the big box
she was hiding behind.

The two kitties cheered.
They picked up the box and posted it
to the most far-off place that
they could think of.

Afterwards, Fluffy decided that she quite liked being a bit grubby and that rolling in muck was fun. And Scruffy agreed that being cleaner and eating delicious food wasn't as bad as he thought.

So Fluffy and Scruffy became friends as well as neighbours . . .

. . . and they never saw any of those grubby little mice ever again.

To Caroline and Genevieve

Scholastic Children's Books
Euston House, 24 Eversholt Street
London NW1 1DB, UK.
A division of Scholastic Ltd
London ~ New York ~ Toronto ~ Sydney ~ Auckland
Mexico City ~ New Delhi ~ Hong Kong

First published in hardback in the UK by Scholastic Ltd, 2006

Copyright © Liz Pichon, 2006

ISBN 0 439 95456 8

All rights reserved

Printed in Singapore

2 4 6 8 10 9 7 5 3 1

The right of Liz Pichon to be identified as the author and illustrator
of this work has been asserted by her in accordance with the
Copyright, Designs and Patents Act, 1988.